ISBN 0-905-114-80-9 (paperback)
ISBN 0-905-114-86-8 (hardback)

Published by Bridge Street Books
LDA Duke Street Wisbech Cambridgeshire PE13 2AE

Desmond had been invited
to a fancy dress garden party.

It was at Beechcroft Hall
the very next day.

Desmond
Please come to a
Fancy Dress Party
in the gardens of
Beechcroft Hall
on Saturday at 3pm
RSVP

Desmond could not think
what to dress up in.
It was very difficult to hide his shape.

Suddenly he had an idea.
'I know. I'll dress up as a dragon.'
he thought.

Desmond told his friend Tom
all about his secret idea.
'I will help you to make
the dragon costume,' said Tom.

They made the body
by stitching lots of green leaves
onto an old sheet
belonging to Desmond.

'It will look just like dragon's scales,'
said Tom.

Tom had another idea.
'I know! I can go as St. George and pretend to kill the dragon with my sword,' he said.

'Please be careful,'
said Desmond.
'It might hurt, being killed.'

'It's all right, my sword
is only a rubber one.
It couldn't hurt anyone,'
said Tom.

They made the dragon's head
and then some armour for Tom
out of cardboard and papier maché.
They had great fun painting them.

'I hope they will be dry
in time for the party tomorrow,'
said Desmond.

The next afternoon they dressed up in their costumes.

'Oh dear,' said Desmond.
'The holes for my eyes are in the wrong place.
I can't see properly.'

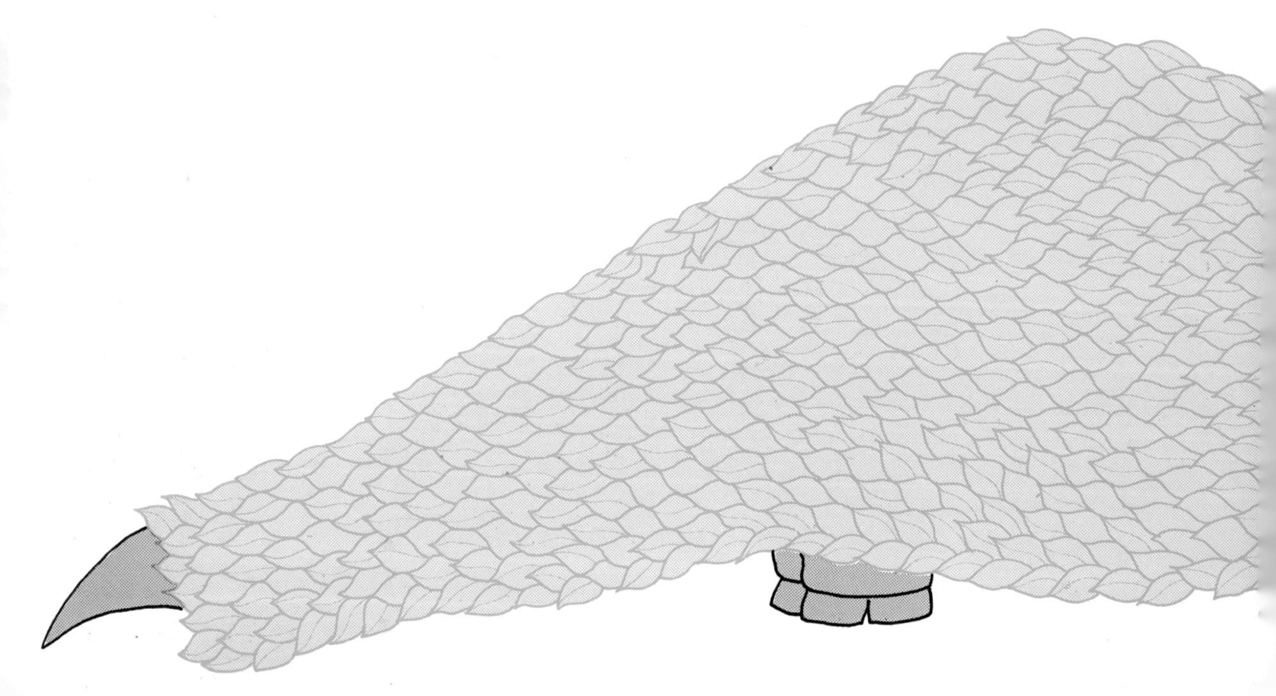

'Don't worry,' said Tom.
'I'll be there to guide you.'

When they got to the party
Tom was so busy looking
at the strange costumes
that he lost sight of Desmond.
Suddenly, there was a great hullabaloo.

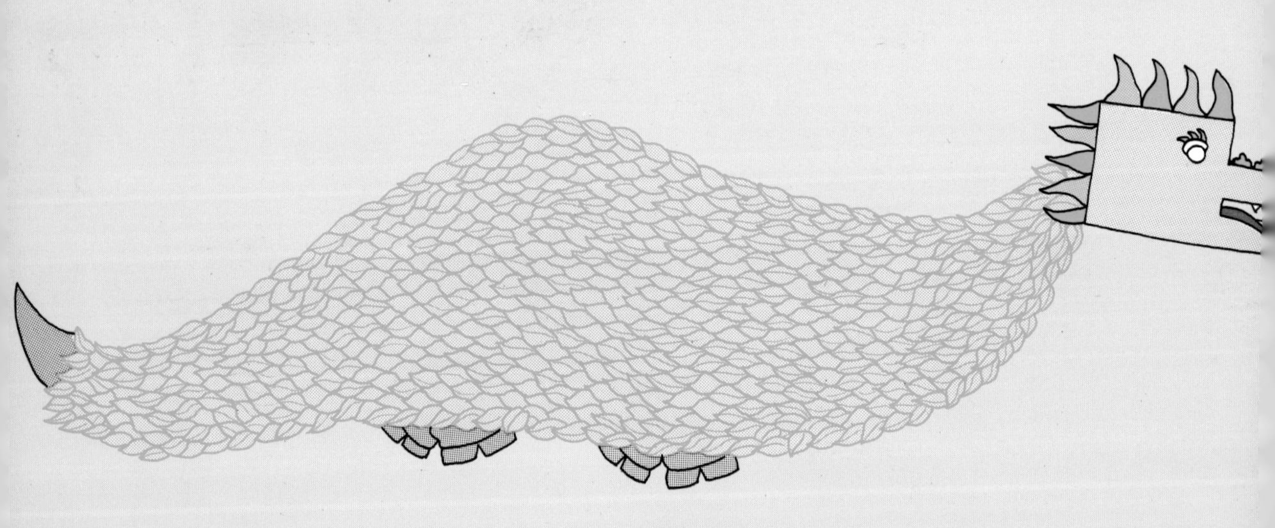

Clowns, witches, bears and policemen were running about, trying to get away from the dragon who was shouting 'Stop, it's all right, it's only me!'

To Tom's horror he saw Desmond,
who couldn't see where he was going,
running straight towards the lake.
Tom rushed after him.
But he was too late.

Splosh! Desmond fell into the water.
'Ooogh! I'm all wet,' he spluttered.

The costume floated off
and there was Desmond
still stuck in the dragon's head.
'Hey!' shouted the other guests.
'It's Desmond the Dinosaur!
How silly of us not to guess.'

They rushed forward to help Desmond
take off the dragon's head
and struggle out of the lake.

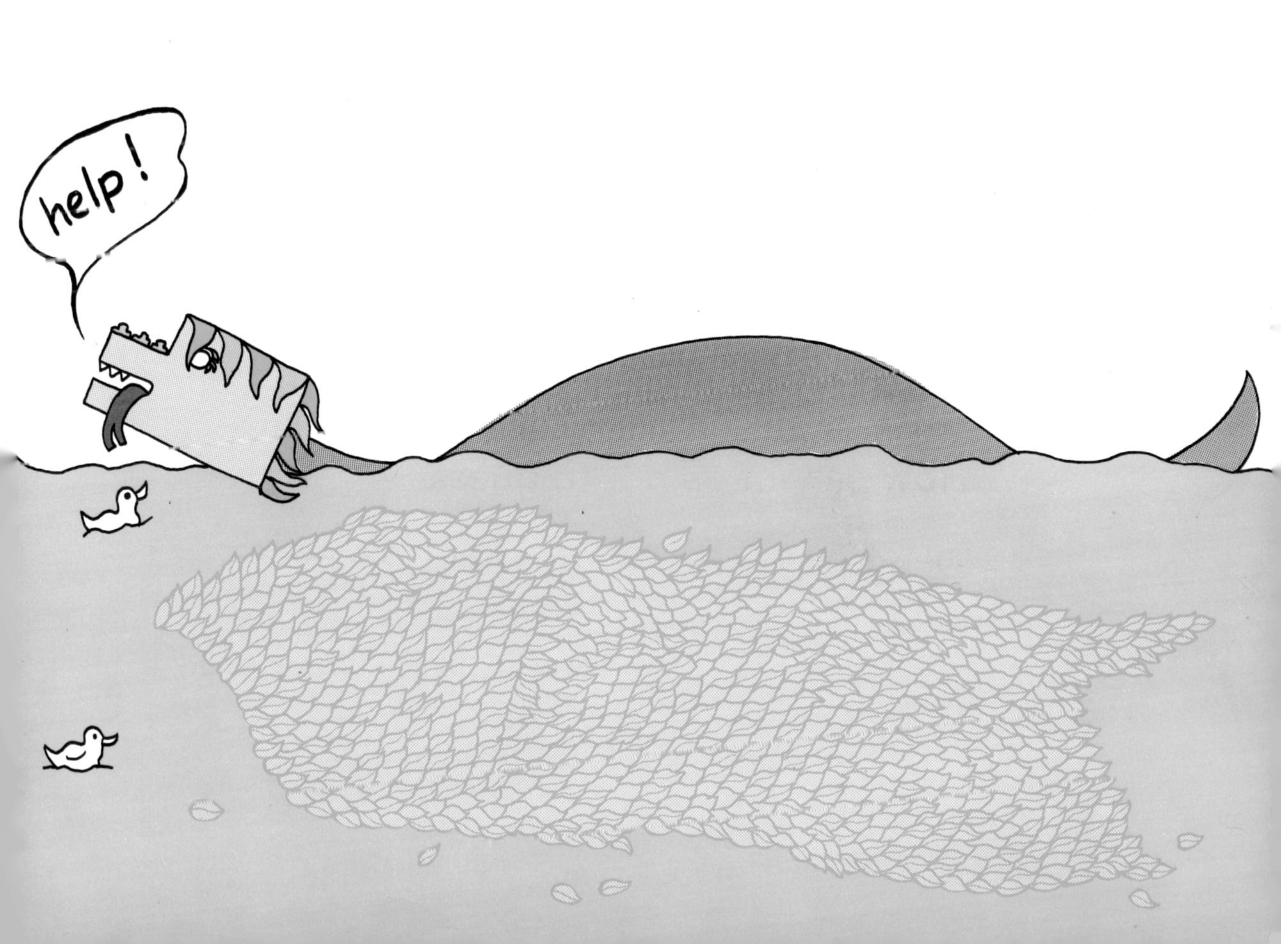
help!

Luckily, the water was quite warm
and Desmond soon dried out in the sun.

Everyone enjoyed the party.
They agreed that Desmond
was quite unusual enough as himself
without dressing up as a dragon.

At the end of the party
Desmond was given a special prize
for having been so fierce
and dragonlike.

'Do let us know
if you are going to dress up
as a dragon again –
you were a bit too frightening!'
they laughed.